M.P. RO ... Jniversity.

He is an in ... :ure books.

His many b ... h the Moon,

The ... e and

For Leo

Hieronymus Betts and his Unusual Pets copyright © Frances Lincoln Limited 2005
Text and illustrations copyright © M.P. Robertson 2005

First published in Great Britain and the USA in 2005 by
Frances Lincoln Children's Books, 4 Torriano Mews,
Torriano Avenue, London NW5 2RZ
www.franceslincoln.com

Distributed in the USA by Publishers Group West

First paperback edition published in Great Britain in 2006 and in the USA in 2007

British Library Cataloguing in Publication Data
available on request

ISBN 10: 1-84507-577-3
ISBN 13: 978-1-84507-577-4

The illustrations are pen and ink and watercolour

Printed in Singapore

3 5 7 9 8 6 4 2

Visit M.P. Robertson's website at **www.mprobertson.com**

Hieronymus Betts
and his Unusual Pets

M.P. Robertson

F

FRANCES LINCOLN
CHILDREN'S BOOKS

Hieronymus Betts has unusual pets.

KEEP DOGS
ON
LEAD

Slurp the slugapotamus is his slimiest pet

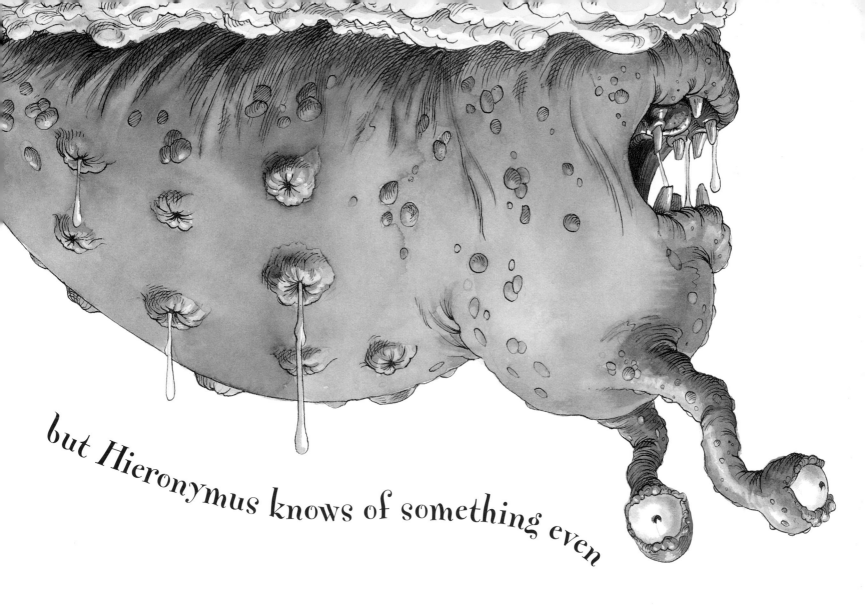

but Hieronymus knows of something even

slimier!

Screech the greater-spotted howler bird
is his noisiest pet

but Hieronymus knows of something even

noisier!

Gobbler the sabre-toothed rhino-toad is his greediest pet

but Hieronymus knows

of something even

greedier!

Cuddles the porcupython
is his scariest pet

but Hieronymus knows

of something even

scarier!

Growler the grizzly hare

is his fiercest pet

but Hieronymus knows of something even

fiercer!

Stinker the bog hog is his smelliest pet

but Hieronymus knows of something even **smellier!**

Oojamaflip the whatchamacallit

is his strangest pet

but Hieronymus knows

of something even

stranger!

So what's **slimier** than a slugapotamus,

noisier than a greater-spotted howler bird,

greedier than a sabre-toothed rhino-toad,

scarier than a porcupython,

fiercer than
a grizzly hare,

smellier than a bog hog,

and **stranger** than
a whatchamacallit?

Dare you turn
this page to find out?

Hieronymus's
little brother –

that's what!

But even though he's

slimier *than*

a slugapotamus,

noisier *than*

a greater-spotted

howler bird,

greedier *than*

a sabre-toothed

rhino-toad,

scarier than a porcupython,

fiercer than a grizzly hare,

smellier than a bog hog,

and stranger than a whatchamacallit...

he's more fun
than any pet could ever be!

MORE TITLES BY M.P. ROBERTSON FROM FRANCES LINCOLN CHILDREN'S BOOKS

The Moon in Swampland

Hidden in the dark, marshy bogs of Swampland,
the wicked and mischievous bogles hide from the Moon,
and lie in wait for travellers. Anyone who wanders too close to the edge
will feel clammy fingers dragging them beneath the murky water.
When the Moon saves a young boy called Thomas, she gets captured
by the bogles and Thomas must set out to save her in return.
Can he end the bogles' reign of terror?

ISBN 1-84507-095-X

Big Foot

One crisp, bright night a little girl hears a sad song. She follows
huge snowy footprints deep into the darkness of the forest.
Cold and shivering, she becomes lost in the falling snow,
far from home. Suddenly, from behind a tree, she spies
a large, hairy face with gentle eyes. It is Big Foot…

ISBN 0-7112-2068-9 (UK)
ISBN 1-84507-153-0 (US)

Seven Ways to Catch the Moon

Have you ever wanted to catch the moon?
You can float through the sky in a hot air balloon,
or ripple through the night on a magic carpet...
Here are seven astonishing moon–catching capers.

ISBN 0-7112-1413-1 (UK)
ISBN 1-84507-231-6 (US)

Frances Lincoln titles are available from all good bookshops.
You can also buy books and find out more about your favourite titles,
authors and illustrators on our website: www.franceslincoln.com